Scarlett's
New
Friend

The Mermaid S.O.S. series

Scarlett's New Friend

gillian shields

illustrated by helen turner

BLOOMSBURY

NEW YORK BERLIN LONDON

Originally published in Great Britain by Bloomsbury Publishing Plc. in 2006
First published in the United States of America in September 2008
by Bloomsbury Books for Young Readers
www.bloomsburykids.com

For information about permission to reproduce selections from this book, write to
Permissions, Bloomsbury BFYR, 175 Fifth Avenue, New York, New York 10010

Library of Congress Cataloging-in-Publication Data
Shields, Gillian.
Scarlett's new friend / Gillian Shields ; illustrated by Helen Turner. — 1st U.S. ed.
p.   cm. — (Mermaid S.O.S. series ; 5)
Summary: The wicked Mantora sets another trap for the young mermaids by littering
a beach where a seal family lives, and Scarlett's bossiness interferes with the clean-up
effort, further delaying the mission to bring the magic crystals home.
ISBN 978-1-59990-255-5
[1. Mermaids—Fiction. 2. Adventure and adventurers—Fiction. 3. Bossiness—Fiction.
4. Seals (Animals)—Fiction. 5. Crabs—Fiction. 6. Litter (Trash)—Fiction.]
I. Turner, Helen. II. Title.
PZ7.S55478Scd 2008   [Fic]—dc22   2008004468

Printed in the U.S.A. by Worldcolor Fairfield, Pennsylvania
2 4 6 8 10 9 7 5 3

For Lois
—G. S.

This book is for my big sisters
Kathleen and Angela, who are
the inspiration for so many
characters yet to be drawn!
All my love —H. T.

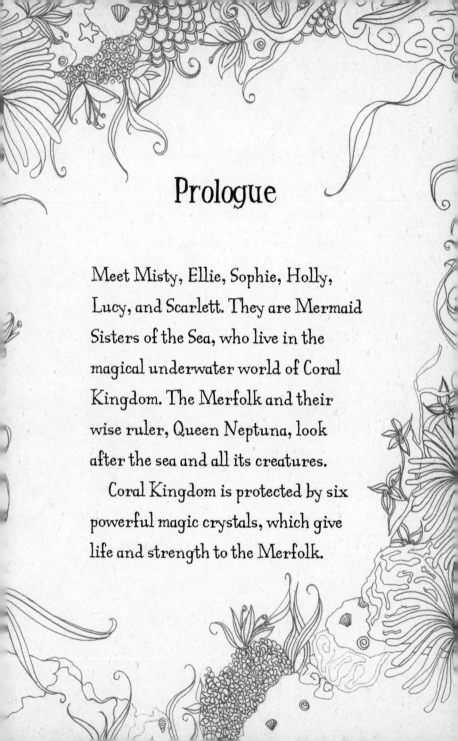

Prologue

Meet Misty, Ellie, Sophie, Holly, Lucy, and Scarlett. They are Mermaid Sisters of the Sea, who live in the magical underwater world of Coral Kingdom. The Merfolk and their wise ruler, Queen Neptuna, look after the sea and all its creatures.

Coral Kingdom is protected by six powerful magic crystals, which give life and strength to the Merfolk.

Without the crystals, Coral Kingdom would not survive.

Every year, the old crystals fade and have to be replaced. Queen Neptuna sends Misty and her friends—six special mermaids who are pure of heart—to collect the new ones from the secret Crystal Cave. But as they are bringing the crystals home, a storm blows the mermaids completely off course.

This is no ordinary storm! It is created by Mantora, Queen Neptuna's jealous sister. Mantora wanted to rule Coral Kingdom, and now she is bitter and full of hatred. She is determined to stop the mermaids from returning home, so that she can overthrow Queen Neptuna and set up her evil Storm Kingdom instead.

Luckily, the young mermaids have courage and friendship on their side. But that's not all; their S.O.S. Kits will help them as they race to get the crystals back safely. And they never forget their Mermaid Pledge:

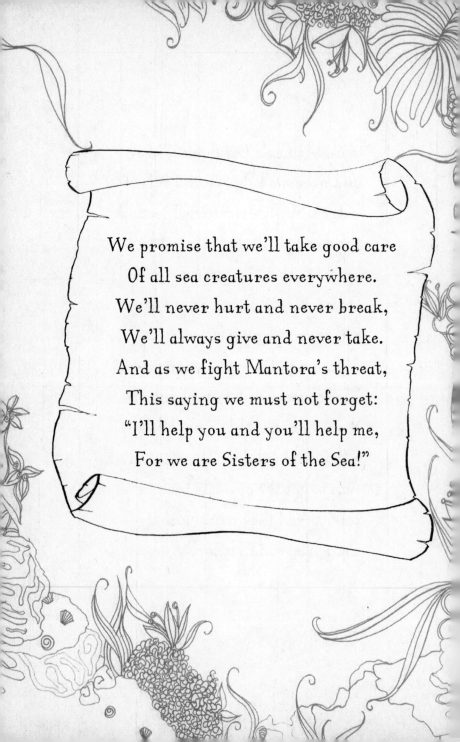

We promise that we'll take good care
Of all sea creatures everywhere.
We'll never hurt and never break,
We'll always give and never take.
And as we fight Mantora's threat,
This saying we must not forget:
"I'll help you and you'll help me,
For we are Sisters of the Sea!"

Scarlett and her friends are eager to prove that Queen Neptuna was right to trust them with the precious crystals. They are going to do everything it takes to get them home and safeguard Coral Kingdom for another year.

Will Mantora win? Or can the mermaids get the new crystals back in time to stop the light fading forever from Coral Kingdom?

Scarlett

Chapter One

Scarlett sped tirelessly through the deep blue water, rippling her spangled crimson tail like a length of red silk. Her long hair streamed out behind her as she dashed along. She and the other mermaids—Misty, Ellie, Sophie, Holly, and Lucy—had been swimming in the fast currents under the sea since the break of day. Every hour that passed brought them closer to home.

"Scarlett," called her friend Sophie, who was just behind her, "could you please swim up to the surface? Have a good look around and see if you recognize where we are."

"All right," replied Scarlett. She was pleased to be asked. At the start of the mermaids' adventures, Scarlett had been a little bit bossy. Now she was learning to work as a team with her Sisters of the Sea.

"Why don't you all rest here for a moment?" she said to the others. "I'll come back right away and tell you what I can see."

The brave young Crystal Keepers had spent the day before searching for long-lost treasure on an ancient shipwreck. Since then, apart from a few hours' rest in the

night, the mermaids had been racing
against time to take the magic crystals
back to Coral Kingdom.

"We've still got today and until sunset
tomorrow to reach home," thought
Scarlett, as she surged upward to the sunlit
surface. "We might just make it—unless

Mantora is planning another nasty surprise to stop us from getting there."

The determined young mermaid cautiously peeped over the waves and looked around carefully. It was a nice, breezy morning.

"I think I've seen that island over there before," she thought to herself. "Perhaps that means we're not too far from Coral Kingdom."

Scarlett shaded her eyes and looked across the dancing waves. A large, green island rose ahead of her. She could make out rocky coves and cliffs and beaches. Human houses clustered round a little harbor. Brightly colored boats were dotted on the sea around the island. A few other smaller islands lay to the North.

"Of course!" she exclaimed to herself. "Wait until I tell the others!"

She leaped for joy above the sparkling sea, her tail glinting like a red flame in the sunlight. Then she plunged beneath the water, to where her friends were waiting just under the waves.

"I've seen it," she shouted. "I've really seen it!"

"What have you seen, Scarlett?" asked Holly. "Are we at Coral Kingdom yet?"

"Not quite," grinned Scarlett, "but we're getting close. I saw Sandy Bay Island ahead of us."

"Sandy Bay Island!" cried Misty. "Then we're nearly there!"

She grabbed Scarlett's hands and spun her around in a wild underwater dance. All the mermaids laughed and sang, "Hooray, hooray, for Sandy Bay!"

Sandy Bay Island was the busy seaside home to many creatures. Gulls, crabs, and seals lived there—and even humans. Beyond the island, further to the West, lay the secret underwater land of Coral

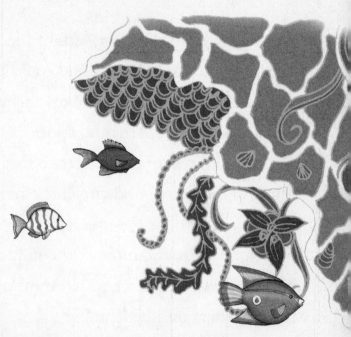

Kingdom. The mermaids really were almost home.

"Now we'll have to be even more careful," warned Scarlett after the celebrations died down. "Mantora might be lurking around nearby. Sandy Bay Island is at least a day's swim from Coral Kingdom. We can't slow down now."

"You're right, Scarlett," said Ellie. "And getting past Sandy Bay Island could be tricky. There are lots of humans there. We don't want to be spotted by them."

"Maybe it would be better to find a place to hide now, and travel the rest of the way after dark?" suggested Lucy quietly. "That way most of the humans will be asleep when we're swimming past their harbors and beaches."

"That's a good idea . . . ," began Scarlett, but she wasn't able to finish what she was going to say. The shadow of a boat passed over the mermaids' heads. A fishing line suddenly whipped down through the water, like a snake. At the end of it was a large hook, which lodged itself into Scarlett's thick hair. Then the unseen human on the

other end of the fishing line began to tug.
He thought he had made a fine catch and
was trying to reel it in.

"Ow!" Scarlett gasped. She tried
frantically to get the hook out of her
hair, and the others desperately
tried to grab her as she
slithered past them. But it
was too late! Scarlett

was being pulled swiftly up to the surface, and soon she would land like a mackerel in the human boat. Where was Scarlett— and her precious crystal—being taken? And how would the other mermaids get her back?

Chapter Two

"Everyone grab hold of Scarlett," shouted
Sophie, as Scarlett hovered above them for
a moment. Holly and Misty caught the
end of Scarlett's tail, but she let out an
agonized squeal.

"Ow, that hurts," she yelped. "I'm being
pulled the other way too. Let go!"

There was nothing the mermaids could
do but watch in horror as Scarlett

disappeared over their heads on the end of
the fishing line.

"We've got to go after her," said Sophie.
"I don't care if the humans do see us.
Come on! *Mermaid S.O.S.!*"

The friends all zoomed up through
the waves to the overwater world. They
were just in time to see Scarlett being
pulled into a small green boat. It was
being handled by a single fisherman
wearing a rough sweater. He had an
honest, weather-beaten face, and he was
clutching the end of his fishing rod with
his mouth hanging wide open. He
looked as surprised as if he had caught
a pot of gold.

The fisherman stared at Scarlett in
amazement, as she sat on her tail opposite

him in the little boat. She angrily unhooked the fishing line from her tangled hair and began to scold him.

"Don't you know that it hurts to be yanked out of the water by a fishing hook?" asked Scarlett fiercely. "How would you like it if I did that to you?"

The magic crystal she was carrying gave

her the power to be understood in any language, even human.

"But . . . but I never meant to catch a . . . a . . . whatever it is you are . . . ," he stuttered.

"Oh, you know perfectly well what I am," said Scarlett. "And all my friends here."

Sophie, Holly, Lucy, Ellie, and Misty were floating in the waves around the boat, watching carefully. Scarlett sounded angry, but they could tell she was a little bit scared too. They were all anxious about being face-to-face with a human like this.

"Well," he said doubtfully, "I guess you're all Merfolk, or my name's not John Roberts. That is, unless I'm dreaming." He rubbed

his eyes and pinched himself. "You're still there, are you? Wait till I tell my boy Jack about this!"

"You will not tell anybody about me and my friends, John Roberts," said Scarlett severely. "Do you really think we want you big clumsy humans coming and staring at us? In fact, I might tip your boat over and send you to the bottom of the sea! That will teach you to go around catching mermaids."

"Oh no, Scarlett," protested Ellie, as she bobbed up and down in the water. "We couldn't do that, not to anyone."

"Remember that the Mermaid Pledge says 'Never hurt,'" said Holly wisely. "That applies to humans too."

"And I don't think this John Roberts creature wants to hurt us, either," added Misty. "Do you?"

"Of course not," John replied quickly. "I've been a fisherman all my life in these waters. So were my father and grandfather, and maybe Jack will be one too. We've never been greedy, only taking from the sea what we needed to live. And we've heard many tales of the Merfolk around here, how they rescued Lady Jane in the old days and so on." He blinked his eyes again in astonishment. "I never believed the stories until now, though young Jack does. But I see now that you're finer than anything in any tale."

"See, Scarlett," said Lucy. "He's sorry for what he did." The mermaids all swam a little closer to the green boat.

"That I am, miss, make no mistake," said John.

"Well, if you're really sorry," said Scarlett slowly, from her narrow bench in the boat, "then I take back those nasty things I said to you. I'll trust you not to trap us like lobsters caught in a pot. And perhaps," she added, "you might even be able to help us."

"But how can a human help a mermaid, Scarlett?" asked Sophie, looking up at her friend.

"I've got an idea about that," Scarlett explained. "We can all see that it's too dangerous to swim past Sandy Bay Island just now. There are lots of small fishing boats, like this one, going in and out of the harbor. And if we swim underwater, we might get caught in the nets of the bigger boats."

"So what's your idea, Scarlett?" asked
Holly.

"I don't see how I can help you," puzzled
John. He still couldn't believe that he was
talking to six mermaids.

"Could you take us in your boat to a
really quiet and secret spot on the Island?"
Scarlett asked him. "If we all crouch
down at the bottom of the boat, no one
will see us. Then we
could stay in
the hiding
place until
the evening.
That's when
most of
you humans
are resting and

it will be safer for us to continue our journey."

"There's Cauldron Cliff on the far side of the Island," replied John thoughtfully. "There's no way down to the beach from the cliff top. And getting there by boat is tricky if you're not used to steering around the rocks. That keeps folks away from it."

"It sounds perfect," said Ellie. "That is, if you wouldn't mind taking us there in your boat, John?"

"Mind?" replied the fisherman. His tanned, open face broke into a broad smile. "Of course I don't mind. It's not every day I get to talk with the Merfolk. Hop in, my dears."

So Holly, Lucy, Misty, Ellie, and Sophie quickly pulled themselves over the side of the faded green boat. Then John hid them under a piece of old sailcloth.

"You'll be safe there," he said. "And it won't take us long to reach Cauldron Cliff."

The mermaids lay quietly as John steered the little boat over the choppy waves. This surely had to be the strangest part of their adventures so far!

Chapter Three

"Here we are," said John. "This is Cauldron Cliff."

Scarlett and her friends peered over the sailcloth that was covering them. They saw a tall, scooped-out cliff, towering above a lonely beach. The cliff really did look a bit like a hollow witch's cauldron. The jagged rocks gleamed purplish-brown, and the pale sand glistened in the midday sunshine. No one was there except for a few seabirds.

"This will be a marvelous hiding place," said Scarlett.

"Thank you, John," said Lucy shyly. "I never believed a human could be so kind."

"And I never believed there were folks like you," he replied. "I can't wait to tell them at home."

"That's the problem," Ellie sighed. "If you told other humans, they might want to capture us. We do like you, John. And we are grateful for your help, but . . ."

"But what?" he asked, with a look of surprise on his face.

"But we can't allow you to remember meeting us," said Scarlett, in a determined voice. "Good-bye, John."

One by one, the mermaids dived into the waves from the boat. They formed a circle around it and began to sing:

You didn't see a mermaid fair,
You didn't catch her by the hair,
You didn't hear our mermaid song,
You'll forget us, before too long.
Go to sleep and drift away,
Forget what you have seen today.
You won't remember seeing me,
And there are no mermaids in the sea!

As they sang, they held up their crystals in front of them. Rays of light flashed out—copper, silver, and gold— which dazzled John's sight. Soon his eyes began to close and his head nodded

onto his chest. He was instantly in a deep sleep.

The mermaids tucked the magic crystals away, and Scarlett silently beckoned the others to swim after her through the turquoise water. They hid carefully behind some low, wet rocks that stretched from the little beach into the sea.

"Lucy, your hair is blowing around in the breeze," whispered Scarlett. "John might see it when he wakes up."

Lucy quickly smoothed down her red curls. The mermaids held hands and held their breath. It was vital to keep out of sight, but they needed to wake John from his enchanted sleep. Softly, like silver chimes on the wind, they called out, "Awake and forget!"

John opened his eyes with a shudder. He looked around, startled and blinking in the sun. The mermaids heard him mutter, "Have I been asleep and drifting in the boat? I've never done that before."

He moved the boat away from the cliff and faced the open sea, but then he quickly looked back over his shoulder. The friends froze behind the rocks as the honest fisherman stared with a puzzled expression toward their hiding place. John seemed to be trying to remember something. He suddenly called out, "Who's there?"

But Cauldron Cliff just echoed his question back to him, "Who's there, who's there, who's there . . . ?" With a last shrug, John turned away. He and his boat were soon out of sight. The mermaids relaxed and breathed again. They slowly swished their gleaming tails and bobbed up and down in the waves that lapped against the rocks.

"As soon as the

humans have gone to sleep," said Scarlett, "we must set off on the last stage of our journey with the crystals. But we'll have to wait here for a while. We can't risk being caught again."

"John was nice, though," said Lucy. "Maybe there are more humans like that."

"I doubt it, Lucy," replied Scarlett. "Don't forget how easily Mantora tricks them into doing what she wants."

"Like cutting down the Kelp Forest," said Misty.

"And spilling oil in the sea," said Ellie.

"And catching dolphins in their fishing nets," said Sophie.

"And letting chemicals leak onto the reef," said Holly.

"And dropping LITTER on the beaches!"

exclaimed Scarlett suddenly. "Have you seen all that trash over there?"

The mermaids swam a little way from the rocks and looked at the lonely beach at the foot of Cauldron Cliff. They gasped with shock. Piles of old newspapers, rusty tin cans, and broken bottles were scattered everywhere.

"How did this happen?" wondered Ellie.

"Oh, I can explain it," said a snuffly sort of voice behind them. Scarlett and her friends whipped around in the water to see who was there. A sleek, friendly seal was perched on the slippery rocks, looking down at them with big, sad eyes.

"I heard you talking about Mantora," he said gloomily. "You're right. That wicked old creature does use the humans to do her

dirty work. But this time she has done the damage all by herself."

"What happened?" said Scarlett urgently. "Has Mantora really been here?"

The seal sighed and his whiskers drooped mournfully. "It's a long story," he replied. "But I will tell you, if you wish."

"Yes, please," said the mermaids. "Tell us all about it."

So he settled himself more comfortably on the rocks in the sunshine, looked solemnly at the mermaids, and began.

what Lori likes best," he continued, "is to come with me to this beach. She looks for bright ribbons of purple seaweed and pure white shells with the other baby seals. And she plays with the mischievous crabs that scamper around these rocks."

"So why do you seem so sad, Scout?" asked Sophie. "This sounds like a happy story."

"I'm coming to the sad part," said Scout darkly. "Early this morning I brought Lori

Chapter Four

"My name is Scout," said the seal. "This spring tide my wife and I had a baby seal. Our Lori is the sweetest little pup on the whole island, if I do say so myself. She has huge dark eyes, plump fur, and soft, smooth flippers."

"She sounds gorgeous," said Scarlett delightedly. "I wish I could see her!"

"Maybe you will," said Scout. "Now,

here to play as usual. But as you can see, someone has dumped piles of garbage onto the sand. And Lori cut her flipper on a big tin can with a jagged edge."

"Oh no!" said the mermaids. "How awful."

"Lori cried and cried," Scout continued, "and I rushed her back to our home beyond the rocks. My poor wife was so frightened when she saw our baby with that great big cut."

"Is Lori all right?" asked Ellie and Lucy anxiously.

"Hopefully the good salt water in the sea will soon heal the cut," replied Scout. "And my wife has wrapped Lori's flipper in a nice piece of kelp for a bandage. But we're still left with all this dangerous litter on our beach—and I can guess who did this!"

"So can we," said Scarlett grimly. "Mantora! She has been following us ever since we set off on our journey for Queen Neptuna, trying to cause trouble for us and our friends."

"But how could Mantora scatter this trash across the beach?" Holly frowned. "She has a tail like us; she can't just walk across the sand—or fly!"

"No, but her black Storm Gulls can,"
said Scout. "I think there was a whole
gang of them here just before dawn,
screeching and yammering away. And
every single one of them carried a piece of
garbage in his beak and let it fall here—
here on this beach where Lori and her
friends love to play."

"That settles it," said Scarlett. "We've

got to clean up this beach so it's safe again for Lori and the other baby seals." Her eyes were bright and her cheeks were pink. She looked like her bossy old self again, determined to get her own way. "Well, what are we waiting for?"

"It seems like a good idea, Scarlett," hesitated Sophie, "but let's not rush into anything. Of course we feel sorry for Lori. But don't forget that we're supposed to be hiding here and staying out of trouble. If we get held up again, we might not get home with the crystals before sunset tomorrow."

"Then everything would be so much worse for Lori and all the sea creatures," said Misty. "Imagine what Mantora would do if she manages to overthrow Queen Neptuna and set up her horrible Storm Kingdom."

"But don't you see?" demanded Scarlett impatiently. "This dirty, dangerous beach is part of Storm Kingdom—right in front of our eyes! It's exactly how Mantora wants it."

Scarlett's friends shivered, as though a cloud had covered the afternoon sun. The littered beach did look sad and ugly. They knew that Mantora would be happy if it stayed like that.

"I think Mantora knew we would swim past Sandy Bay Island," Scarlett went on, "and she did this to show us her power."

"And to slow us down on our journey," added Ellie, looking around unhappily. "Oh, what should we do?"

"If we really want to fight Mantora, we've got to clean up this beach," declared Scarlett, with a stubborn expression on her face.

The other mermaids glanced at each other uncertainly. It was impossible to say no to Scarlett when she was in this bossy mood.

"But, Scarlett, how could we get across the beach to pick up the litter?" asked Sophie.

"We'll just have to find some other creatures to help us," replied Scarlett. "I'm sure it won't be too hard."

"Well, all right then," said Holly slowly. "We all want to help clean the beach. But we must be careful and keep our crystals safe. We don't want anything to delay our journey home tonight."

Scout looked very pleased. "I'll go and tell Lori," he said. "She'll be so happy."

The father seal dived clumsily from the
rocks and then streamed away under
the water.

Scarlett quickly started to tell the other
mermaids her ideas for cleaning the beach.

"We can't take the trash away
anywhere," she said, "so the best thing
to do is to bury it."

"How will we do that?" asked Sophie.

"It's simple," explained Scarlett. "We'll

swim over from these rocks and sit at the water's edge. The tide is low at the moment, so we'll scoop out some holes in the damp sand with the scallop shells in our S.O.S. Kits. The holes will be our garbage pits. We'll fill them up with the litter and cover it carefully with pebbles. When the tide comes in later, everything will be completely hidden."

"So who should we ask to help us, Scarlett?" wondered Ellie. "We can't walk over the beach to pick things up."

"We have friends with beaks and wings, though," replied Scarlett determinedly. "You can ask the seabirds to help."

Soon the mermaids were sitting on their curling tails by the edge of the shore. Ellie made the special bird call that the great

albatross had taught her, while Scarlett decided where to dig the holes in the sand. In a few moments, some seabirds with long legs and beaks gathered by the water's edge. They were waders, and they had heard Ellie's call.

"We will help you," said the waders, in their quick, chirruping voices.

"Excellent," said Scarlett. "Show them what to do, Ellie, and I'll get some more help. Didn't Scout say that there were lots of crabs on this beach? Their scurrying legs and snapping pincers will be just right for picking up litter."

She shook her long hair back from her face and cupped her hands around her mouth.

"All crabs must report for duty NOW, in the name of Queen Neptuna," she called. "I've got a job for you!"

Chapter Five

A group of curious young pebble crabs
lined up in a row in front of Scarlett.
They had pinky-orange shells and large
front claws.

"Okay," she said briskly, "you crabs are
going to help us. We've got to get this
beach cleaned up so that Lori and the
other baby seals can play here safely."

"Why should we do all the work?" asked

one of them, stepping
forward boldly. "It's
not our problem!"

"It will be your
problem if I tell
Queen Neptuna that
you refused to help us," said Scarlett
angrily. "What's your name?"

"I'm not telling you, bossy boots," said
the fearless crab.

"Ooh, Buster," giggled the other pebble
crabs, "you'll make her so mad!"

"So it's Buster, is it?" said Scarlett, her
cheeks burning with annoyance. "Well,
Buster, you and your friends had better
get to work if you don't want to be
reported to Her Majesty when we get back
to Coral Kingdom."

Sophie and the other mermaids glanced at each other nervously. Scarlett was being so bossy—and just when she had been learning to be more patient and gentle. The young friends didn't think this was the right way to persuade the crabs to help. But Scarlett was so eager to clear up the beach that she wasn't in the mood to listen to their advice.

Buster just muttered sulkily and fell

back into line. He didn't dare argue with Scarlett—nobody did!

Soon the pebble crabs were scurrying over the beach. They collected scraps of newspaper and bottle tops in their agile pincers and put them in big heaps at the water's edge. Ellie asked the waders to pick up the larger pieces of garbage in their strong beaks, as they stepped over the sand on their elegant legs.

The mermaids took off their delicate shell bracelets, so that they wouldn't get dirty, and put them carefully on top of a big, half-buried rock. It stuck out at the edge of the shore where the friends were sitting. Then they scooped out deep, damp holes in the sand. Scarlett began to fill the holes with the trash collected by the crabs and seabirds.

After everyone had worked hard for a long time, Scarlett looked around. The beach was starting to look much better. Curling fronds of fresh green seaweed emerged from underneath the tattered old newspapers. Tin cans and broken bottles no longer hid the pearly shells that lay on the glittering white sand. The mermaids and their helpers were doing a good job. But the crabs were slowing down.

"Can't we rest?" groaned Buster. "My pincers are nearly falling off from carting all that stuff over here."

"Don't be silly," said Scarlett. "Carrying a few bits and pieces won't hurt you. Look at these big holes we had to dig. That really did make our arms ache."

Some of the other pebble crabs also muttered about wanting to rest. They took a break from work and started to play a game with the mermaids' colorful bracelets, throwing them high in the air and seizing them with their hooked claws.

"Stop messing around with our stuff," called Scarlett indignantly. "Put them down and get back to your jobs!"

Sophie was beginning to wonder if she should ask Scarlett not to be so bossy. But before she could say anything, Scarlett was busy giving out more instructions.

"We need to fill up all the holes," she said eagerly, "before the tide comes in. Come on, everyone! Think how excited Lori will be when she sees the beach clean and the sand glistening again."

Scarlett was trying so hard to please the injured baby seal that she didn't notice that the crabs were not pleased at all! They grumbled under their breath as they dragged the last few bits of litter over to the mermaids. Then everything was covered over with pebbles.

"There!" said Scarlett at last. "Now the holes are full and the evening tide is coming in to hide them. No one would ever know that there had ever been any trash here at all."

The mermaids looked around the newly cleaned beach with satisfaction.

"Thank you for your help, my seabird friends," called Ellie. The waders folded up their long legs as they flew away, chirruping in farewell.

"I'm going to tell Scout that he can bring Lori to see what we've done," said Scarlett excitedly. "I can't wait to meet her!"

She was about to slip into the water to find the seals when Sophie said, ". . . Er . . . don't you think you should say 'thank you' to the crabs, Scarlett?"

"What do you mean?" asked Scarlett, over her shoulder. "Oh . . . um . . . yes. Thanks!"

Then she dived into the sea, her red tail
reflecting the rosy evening sun.

"The nerve!" said Buster. "Come on,
friends, let's get home while she's gone.
Otherwise, she'll have us working all
night long."

"Thank you for helping," the mermaids
chorused. Buster and his gang scuttled
into the waves on their sharp claws,
leaving a long trail behind them in the

glistening sand. The crabs were eager to get back to their underwater homes for a well-earned rest.

"Oh dear," said Misty, "I know Scarlett has done a great job getting everyone to clean up the beach, but . . ."

". . . but Sisters of the Sea have to learn to say 'please' and 'thank you' and work as a team," finished Holly.

"Well, I think we're all learning a lot on our journey," said Sophie. "I'm sure Scarlett will soon learn that lesson too. Here she comes."

"And look," cried Lucy, "that must be Lori!"

Scarlett sat at the edge of the shore and proudly showed the beach to her new friend Lori, the little seal pup with the

bandaged flipper. The rocks and seaweeds
and shells gleamed brightly in the sunset's
warm glow. Lori waddled carefully onto
the pure, silvery sand, followed closely
by Scout.

"Isn't it great, Dad?" said Lori excitedly.

"I can come and play here with my friends tomorrow. Scarlett has done all this for us. She's my new best friend!"

"That's wonderful," beamed Scout. "But now it's time for baby seals to go to sleep."

"And it's time for us to be on our way to Coral Kingdom," said Holly.

"Yes, the humans will be going to sleep, too," said Ellie. "It should be safe now for us to swim past their harbors and homes."

"Is everyone ready?" asked Misty, as Scarlett cuddled Lori good-bye, and the mermaids gathered their bracelets from where they had left them on the big rock.

"Just a minute," said Scarlett, "I need to collect my things."

She searched by the rock for a few

moments then turned to her friends with
wide, worried eyes.

"What's wrong?" Sophie asked.

"Oh, Sophie," wailed Scarlett. "I can't
find my crystal!"

Chapter Six

All the mermaids looked in astonishment at Scarlett's shocked, pale face.

"I took off my pouch before we started cleaning up," she explained miserably. "I put it out of the way on that big rock, because I didn't want to get it dirty when we were digging. But the pouch isn't there anymore."

"Has it been knocked off into the sea by the waves?" asked Holly.

"No, I'm sure it hasn't," replied Scarlett. "There's a sharp part on the top of that rock. It sticks up like a branch of coral. I tied my pouch onto it very carefully."

"So it couldn't have been washed away by accident?" said Ellie.

"Definitely not," said Scarlett. "Someone must have taken it!"

"But who would have done that?" asked

Lucy. "No one has been here except us, and the waders. Oh, and the pebble crabs, of course."

The other mermaids looked up hesitantly.

"Er . . . Scarlett," said Sophie, "you know that we're good friends. So you won't mind me saying that you were a little bit, well, bossy to those young crabs."

"Was I?" asked Scarlett, with a worried expression. "It's just that the beach was such a mess. Getting it cleaned up as quickly as possible seemed like the most important thing in the world. I suppose I got a little carried away. But I didn't mean to be bossy." She hid her face unhappily in her long silky curls.

"We know that," said Sophie kindly. "But I think the crabs were fed up that you

didn't say 'thank you' to them properly. So maybe . . ."

". . . maybe," Holly worked out, "they took your pouch just to tease you? The crabs were playing with our bracelets earlier, and they knew you'd be angry if they messed around with your things."

"That naughty Buster has probably just hidden your pouch as a joke," added Misty.

"He didn't know there was something really important in it."

"Something really important!" groaned Scarlett. "It's the most important thing in the whole world. We've come so far, but now we won't be able to get all the crystals home in time. And it's because of my stupid bossiness." She started to cry. Misty quickly explained to the seals about the crystals.

"Don't cry," said Lori, nuzzling Scarlett. "I cried when I hurt my flipper, but it's getting better now. And we'll make you better!"

"I know you want to help, Lori," sniffed Scarlett. "But I don't see how you can."

"Didn't I tell you that Lori always plays with those crabs?" said Scout. "We know them well, and taking your pouch for a silly joke is just the kind of trick they would play. We'll help you get it back from them."

"Would you really?" asked Scarlett, wiping her tears away. "I don't deserve it."

"Of course you do," smiled Scout. "You made a big effort to clean the beach, even if you did make a mistake. It's not making the same one twice that's important!"

"I will never, never be bossy again," vowed Scarlett. Then she smiled weakly. "At least, I'll try not to be."

"Here's my

plan," said Scout. "The sun has set, so all
the crabs will be asleep now, tucked away
under the rocks on the seabed. But as soon
as the dawn wakes them, Lori will ask
them very nicely to give your pouch back.
I'm sure that tricky little Buster is at the
bottom of this."

The mermaids thanked the seals and
watched them splash away to their home.
Then they tried to settle down for the night,
hidden behind the rocks on the shore.

As the faraway stars flickered in the
darkening sky, the young friends felt very
worried. They hoped that Scout was right,
but even if they did get the crystal back at
dawn the next day, would there be enough
time to reach Coral Kingdom before sunset?
And would it be dangerous to swim past

Sandy Bay Island in the early morning?
There seemed to be so many problems . . .

At last, they fell into an uneasy sleep.
Only Scarlett was still awake, staring up at
the ghostly moon. She went over everything
in her mind, again and again, wishing she
could unsay all her thoughtless words. She
would never forgive herself if their whole
mission failed because of her. After a long
time, Scarlett dozed fretfully. In her dreams,
it seemed that Queen Neptuna's clear voice

was calling to her from a long way off: "I trust you with this task, my dear young Sisters of the Sea!"

Scarlett woke up suddenly, as though she had been summoned by a distant bell. It was the strange, silent moment before the dawn. Somehow, she would prove that the Queen had been right to trust her!

Without disturbing the others, Scarlett slipped into the cool, gleaming waves. Then, with a flick of her shimmering tail, she

swam down to the seabed where Buster and his friends would just be waking up. She glided around the bottom of the shadowy rocks, past the waving sea anemones. Soon, she saw a group of little crabs starting to stir on the pale, sandy floor.

"Excuse me, please," she said politely. "I just came to say thank you for helping to clean the beach yesterday. And another thing . . ." She took a deep breath and added, "I'm very, very sorry I was so bossy. I know that it was wrong."

The crabs all looked up at her in surprise.

"Wait until Buster hears this," they squeaked. Just then, a little pair of eyes peeped out from a crack in the rock, followed by some scuttling claws. It was Buster himself.

"I've done something wrong too," he said firmly. He dived back into the dark crack and then came out again, dragging

Scarlett's missing red pouch behind him. "I was angry, so I took your pouch to tease you. But I know you just wanted to make the beach nice. Here you are."

He handed over the pouch. Scarlett quickly opened it with a beating heart. The irreplaceable crystal glittered safely inside, like an underwater star! She took it out and held it thankfully.

"So next time you want help cleaning up a beach, you only have to say 'please,'" said Buster with a mischievous grin. "After all, friends are there to help."

"I will," laughed Scarlett. "And we really are friends now—promise?"

"We promise," cried the pebble crabs, waving their curving claws, as Scarlett sped up through the clear morning sea.

She swam joyfully back to the rocks, where the other mermaids were starting to open their eyes and stretch their arms.

"I've got my crystal," Scarlett cried, holding it up for them to see its sparkling rays. "We can begin our journey home."

"That was fast," said Scout, who had just arrived at the rocks with Lori.

"It was easy in the end," smiled Scarlett.

"Saying 'please' and 'thank you'—and 'sorry'—isn't so hard when you're with friends."

Scarlett turned to the baby seal. "We'll always be friends too," she said. Then she gently touched Lori's injured flipper with the gleaming crystal. Lori shook off the kelp bandage and looked in amazement at where the cut had been.

"It's gone," she squeaked gratefully.
"You've healed it."

"So now there's nothing to stop us
swimming straight to Coral Kingdom,"
said Misty.

"Nothing at all—except maybe
Mantora," said Scarlett with a shiver. It
was a scary thought. The mermaids had
gotten so close to Coral Kingdom, but
they knew that Mantora would still be
plotting viciously against them,
desperate to spoil their plans. Now,
every single moment was precious.
After a quick hug with the adorable
baby seal, the brave young friends got
ready to set off on the final stage of
their great journey.

"Good-bye, Scout. Good-bye, little Lori,"

Scarlett cried, as she put away her crystal carefully.

"Come on, mermaids," said Sophie. "Let's race for home!"

The Sisters of the Sea plunged into the waves and surged swiftly away from Cauldron Cliff, as the sun rose higher in the sky like a bright, golden jewel. It was

the very last day of the mermaids' adventures with the crystals, and there was only one question in their minds and hearts.

Would they get to Coral Kingdom in time—or would Mantora finally destroy all their hopes and dreams before sunset that night? The brave young mermaids would soon find out . . .

Mermaid Sisters of the Sea

Misty has flowing blonde hair and a shimmering pink tail. Misty is a really determined and brave mermaid.

Ellie is very caring and loves seabirds. She has long, wavy dark hair and a glittering purple tail.

Sophie has funky fair hair and a blazing, bright orange tail, which helps her to swim super fast.

Holly has sweet, short black hair and a dazzling yellow tail. Holly is very thoughtful and clever.

Scarlett has fabulous, thick dark hair and a gleaming red tail. She can be a little bit bossy and headstrong sometimes.

Lucy has fiery red hair and an emerald green tail, but don't let that fool you—she is really quite shy.

Read all the books in the Mermaid S.O.S. series!

Misty to the Rescue

gillian shields

Ellie and the Secret Potion

gillian shields

Sophie Makes a Splash

gillian shields

Holly Takes a Risk

gillian shields

Scarlett's New Friend

gillian shields

Lucy and the Magic Crystal

gillian shields